**FRILLBACK**
super strong!

**GRANDPOUTER**
squad leader!

**TRENT**
pet twig

**ROCK**
master of disguise!

# CONTENTS

'Mmm...!'

PART ONE

# THE NEST THIEF

# CHAPTER 1

Rock Pigeon is sitting in a shoe.

Is he trying to rest?

Or pretending to be a human ankle?

'It's a bit cold – I should put a sock on!'

Or hoping the shoe turns into a car?

In fact, Rock is in a shoe that's hanging from a power line.

He's waiting for someone.

Along with the entire **REAL PIGEONS** squad.

'How much longer?'

'Not long.'

'I'm getting shoe stink on my feathery curls!'

'You birds should have brought snacks!'

'Stay alert, squad!'

Finally, a man
walks below them.

He stole a puppy earlier. Now it's time for justice.

The **REAL PIGEONS** get to work.

They chew through the shoelaces holding them up and . . .

FALL DOWN.

The pigeons do one of their favourite attack moves – **FLY KICKS!**

Rock **BOOTS** the man in the bottom.

While Frillback grabs the sack.

The puppy is returned.

The **REAL PIGEONS** save the day again.

They go back to their gazebo. But something worse than a puppy-stealer is waiting for them.

'**HULLO, PIGEONS!**'

It's a vulture!

**AHHHHHHHH!**

'He's terrifying and also loud!'

'I've been watching you all,' booms the vulture. 'You're the **REAL PIGEONS**, aren't you?'

Rock leaps back in fright.

WIGGLE

WIGGLE

He has heard scary things about vultures. They are **OMENS OF DOOM!**

But Rock is too tangled up to flap his wings.

He lands hard on the ground.

THWACK!

Frillback raises her feather fists.

'Stay where you are, SCARY VULTURE!'

Rock's wing hurts.

'Ouch!'

'Be brave, DUDE!'

Grandpouter bandages it with the help of Trent, Rock's favourite twig. 'It's just a sprain,' he says. 'No more costumes for a while, though.'

'But being a MASTER OF DISGUISE is my PIGEON POWER!'

The vulture lands beside them.

'Sorry you had a
# WING DING!'
he booms.

### 'I'M BEARDY VULTURE.
I've been looking
for you because –'

'I know all about vultures!' shouts Rock.
'You are **OMENS OF DOOM**. You must
have **CURSED** me and made me fall!'

'Huh?'

'Don't play dumb,' says Grandpouter.
'Everyone knows vultures are scary
birds who **CURSE** and eat **BONES**.'

Beardy Vulture laughs loudly. 'It's true, I do love eating bones.'

bone broth

bone fairy floss

bone hot dog

'But I'm not here to curse anyone,' he adds. 'I've come to report a crime. Someone has stolen my nest. Can you **BELIEVE** it?'

Rock raises an eyebrow. 'Who would steal a vulture's nest?'

'A HUMAN,' says the vulture. 'She hiked up to my mountain. And stole my nest while I was out for dinner. SO NAUGHTY! I followed her back to a house in the city. But I'm too big to sneak inside.'

'I want my nest back,' adds Beardy Vulture.
'I spent ages making it extra big so I can sleep
in it spread-eagled!'

'So will you take the case?
# PLEEEEASE?'

The vulture **SAYS** he's not there to
curse the **REAL PIGEONS**. But he
still **LOOKS** like a scary bone-eater.
And Rock's wing really hurts.

If they don't take the case,
the vulture might still **CURSE** them.
There is only one thing to do.

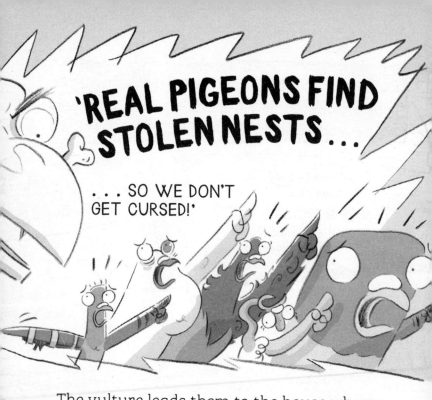

# 'REAL PIGEONS FIND STOLEN NESTS...

### ... SO WE DON'T GET CURSED!'

The vulture leads them to the house where the nest was taken.

'Here's the plan,' says Grandpouter on the way. 'We get inside, we grab the nest, we get out!'

It sounds simple. But the pigeons have never rescued a **NEST** before. And Rock can't use his **PIGEON POWER**.

They arrive at the house, where there is already a problem. There is a **PARTY** on!

'Welcome to Lady Twitcher's mansion,' says a security guard.

'Please have your invites ready!'

JACKIE'S BIRTHDAY BASH

fancy

fancy

fancy

One pigeon could sneak inside. But a whole squad would freak the humans out.

'We'll have to wear disguises,' says Frillback.

'Good luck,' says the vulture, flying off. 'Don't come back without my nest!'

Some humans wander past with dogs in handbags.

'Hello, **DOGS!**' says Homey.

'Why are you in handbags?'

'Because handbags are hammocks that move!'

'Maybe I can disguise myself as a **DOG**,' cries Homey.

He dives into one of the handbags and finds some socks and a stick of eyeliner. His disguise isn't very good, but it will do.

'Woof, doggo!'

The other **REAL PIGEONS** disguise themselves too.

dog

dress

shoelace

wheels

Except for Rock. He feels naked without a disguise of his own. Probably because he **IS** naked. Most pigeons are.

The humans start going inside and the pigeons move with them. Their disguises are working!

Rock doesn't want to be left out of the mission. He decides to just make a run for it.

Luckily no-one sees him.

'Go Rock, go!'

When the **REAL PIGEONS** get inside the mansion, they see that someone is greeting the guests.

A tall woman in a massive, feathery coat. This must be Lady Twitcher. She looks like she's dressed in chickens.

'Tweet! Tweet!'
says Lady Twitcher.

'Welcome to the party, tweeties! Come in and see my amazing new ...'

And Beardy's stolen nest!

It's huge and awesome and covered in chains ... and a padlock.

'There's our target, squad!' says Grandpouter. 'But how on earth will we steal it back?'

# CHAPTER 2

Rock can't stop staring at the nest. It is **AMAZING**. But he is about to get squashed.

So he flies straight into the nearest hiding spot.

Beards are a great place to hide **AND** watch.

'**PSST!**' Rock whispers.

**PSST** is a secret pigeon code.
It means – **P**igeons
            **S**hould
            **S**ee
            **T**his!

The **REAL PIGEONS** notice
and sneak into the beard too.

All except Homey, who is enjoying life as a dog.

'I had no idea bread slices could be so thin!'

TISSUES

The **REAL PIGEONS** look at the nest.

'Lady Twitcher must want to be a bird,' says Rock. 'Otherwise why would she steal a nest? I'll bet she sleeps in it at night.'

'Those chains look too strong for me,' says Frillback, worried.

'Is there something **IN** the nest?' says Rock.

Suddenly a bird flies out of the nest and across the room. She lands on Lady Twitcher's head.

'Why, it's my Jacobin Pigeon! Hello, Jackie!'

'WOW!'

'Look at her beautiful feathers!'

The bird is a beautiful **PIGEON** who looks just like Lady Twitcher! How strange.

'**TWEET TWEET!** May I have your attention,' says Lady Twitcher.

She smiles at Jackie Pigeon.

'Thank you for coming to Jackie's birthday party!' Lady Twitcher says. 'I know I'm a bit mad, throwing a party for my pet bird. But I love her! That's why I got her this beautiful nest for a present.'

'It looks so coo!' says Tumbler.

'Vulture nests are rare and expensive,'
Lady Twitcher continues. 'My security guard,
Reginald, will keep it safe.'

'That's right,' says Reginald. 'This nest is
chained down and only I have the key!'

Rock gulps. Chains, a padlock **and** a guard.
The nest is going to be really hard to steal
back.

'If we can't get the nest, the vulture
will **CURSE** all of us,' says Frillback.
'He'll probably straighten out my curls!'

At that moment, all the dogs – and Homey – start to vomit.

'Sorry, DOG PALS! I guess those thin slices weren't bread after all.'

little tissue vomits →

'OWWWWW!' says Lady Twitcher. 'I mean ... EWWWW!'

Lady Twitcher looks at Jackie strangely. When she speaks, her voice sounds very pinched.

'Attention everyone,' says Lady Twitcher tightly. 'Please put your dogs in the doggy bed. Before they make any more mess. Jackie doesn't like it.'

The humans dump their dogs in the big, round doggy bed in the corner. Homey ditches his costume and flies into the beard.

'Why don't I just throw these mutts into the backyard?' growls Reginald.

He picks up the dogs, bed and all.

'Uh . . . no, they can stay,' says Lady Twitcher. 'We shouldn't be too mean to the animals. Should we, Jackie?'

While Reginald is talking to Lady Twitcher, Tumbler makes a move.

'Tumbler! Where are you going?'

She moulds herself into the key shape.

Then flies back into the beard.

# Tumbler is a genius.

She's like a photocopier for keys!

'Now we can unlock that padlock with **ME!**' she smiles.

'After that, we can pull the chains off,' says Rock. 'But then what?'

'We could take the nest out through the fireplace,' says Frillback. 'If it fits!'

'We'll just need to find out where that fireplace leads,' says Grandpouter. 'There must be a chimney outside!'

'Now we need to get out of this beard without being seen,' says Tumbler. 'But how?'

32

Frillback has an idea.

'I'll make this man walk us out.'

She dives down into the man's clothes.

And wriggles around.

Until he can't stand it any more. And leaves the room.

'Excuse me!'

The man arrives in an empty hallway and the pigeons fly out.

'Pigeons in my beard? Again?'

The pigeons find a back door.

'Let's go out to find the chimney PIGS . . . er, I mean PIGeons!'

says Homey.

34

Rock's wing still hurts, so Homey waits with him in the backyard. The others go looking for the right chimney.

'Time for a rest,' says Rock.

He flies over to an old barbecue to perch.

'HULLO?' cries a voice from below.

Rock is so startled he falls off the barbecue.

Is he about to hurt his wing – again?

# CHAPTER 3

Luckily, Homey catches Rock this time.

'Gotcha, dude!'

Beardy Vulture was under the lid of the barbecue.

'Sorry to scare you again – I was having a nap,'

says Beardy.

'You are a tad JUMPY, though. Haha!'

Rock frowns at Beardy Vulture.

'I can't believe you tried to **CURSE** me again!' he says.

Homey bravely leaps onto the vulture.

'I'm putting you under Homey Arrest!' he says.

'For **CURSING** my buddy Rock!'

'Looks like you're hugging me more than arresting me!'

Rock is **mad**.

But it turns out, so is Beardy Vulture.

He stamps his talons. 'I have **NEVER CURSED** anyone in my life,' he shouts.

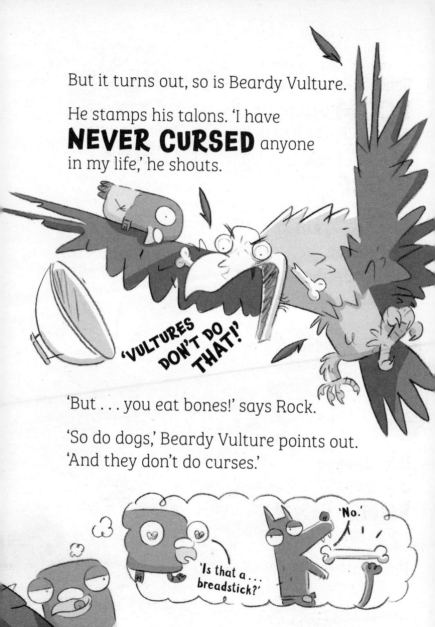

'VULTURES DON'T DO THAT!'

'But . . . you eat bones!' says Rock.

'So do dogs,' Beardy Vulture points out. 'And they don't do curses.'

'Is that a . . . breadstick?'

'No.'

'That's true,' admits Homey.

'Everyone says that we're **OMENS OF DOOM** because we look scary!' explains Beardy. 'I'm sick of it. I'm just a vulture with a heart of gold and a good **OUTSIDE VOICE**.'

'Hullo, neighbour!'

'Howdy!'

Beardy picks a sunflower from the garden and gives it to Rock. 'I'm sorry about your **WING DING**. But I didn't **CURSE** you. I accidentally scared you, that's all.'

Rock thinks the flower is beautiful.

'Thank you, Beardy Vulture.'

Rock realises he has misunderstood Beardy. This vulture might be loud and scary-looking on the outside. But he's **SWEET** on the inside.

'Does this mean we're friends with Beardy now?' asks Homey.

'Yeah!' says Rock.

'Then it's a good thing I'm already hugging him,' says Homey.

Beardy smiles. 'Now listen, I've found a clue. I know where Lady Twitcher lives.'

'We **ALL** know that, dude!' says Homey.

Beardy Vulture shakes his head. 'No, she doesn't live in the mansion. She lives in that **SHED!** Can you **BELIEVE** it?'

They walk over to the shed.
The door is slightly ajar.

They step inside.

There are books and papers everywhere.

The walls are covered with bird paintings.

Whoever lives here really loves birds.

BIRD BAKERY

'Look! A bakery run by birds,' says Homey. 'Awesome!'

Rock scratches his chin. Why would Lady Twitcher live out here when she has a huge house?

'Hello, common birds!' says a voice.

It is Lady Twitcher's pet pigeon.

'Hi, Jackie,' says Rock, surprised. 'We're the **REAL PIGEONS** and we're here to take back the vulture's stolen nest.'

Then Rock looks closer.

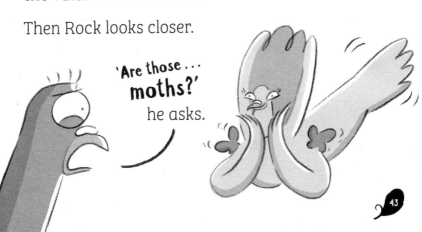

'Are those . . . **moths?**' he asks.

'Yes, my moths carry me places,' says Jackie Pigeon. 'I am a **QUEEN**. And a true **QUEEN** does not flap her own wings.'

'You're a queen?' says Beardy doubtfully.

'Yes!' she sneers. 'I **LOOK** like one, don't I?'

'I thought you were Lady Twitcher's pet,' Rock says, uneasily.

'I'm not her pet,' Jackie laughs. 'Lady Twitcher is **MY** pet! I made her throw me this birthday party. I control **EVERYTHING** she does!'

'*How?*' asks Rock.

Jackie thrusts out her claws. They are super long and razor sharp.

'I sit on her head and dig in my claws until she does what I want,' Jackie says.

'Giving painful pinches is my **PIGEON POWER!**'

45

Lady Twitcher isn't a human who thinks she's a bird.

She's just under the control of an EVIL PIGEON!

'Claws are **NOT** for pinching people!' cries Rock. 'Claws are for walking. And carrying breadcrumbs. And doing **SPIDER SHADOW-PUPPET SHOWS!**'

But Jackie smiles. Her eyes are like daggers. 'You'll never make shadow puppets again!' she says. 'Because I'm going to end you. And stop you from stealing my beautiful nest.'

Jackie waves at her moths.

Rock and Homey shrink back. Jackie might look beautiful, but really she is SCARY and MEAN.

'I'm going to PINCH you to pieces,' she sneers.

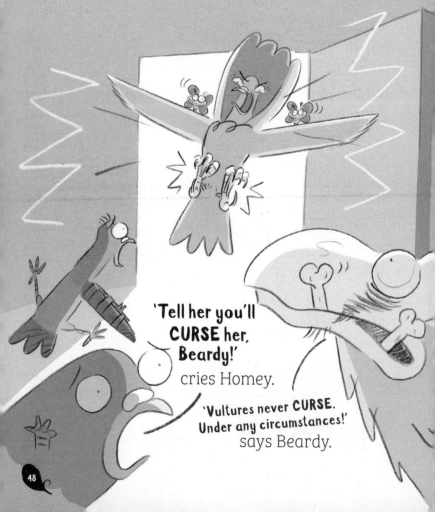

'Tell her you'll CURSE her, Beardy!' cries Homey.

'Vultures never CURSE. Under any circumstances!' says Beardy.

'We do have other skills, though.' Beardy spits a bone towards the wall.

The bone hits a switch and a light comes on.

The moths suddenly change direction and fly towards the light.

Moths can't resist bright lights.

While Jackie tries to get her moths to turn around, Rock, Homey and Beardy burst out of the shed and escape.

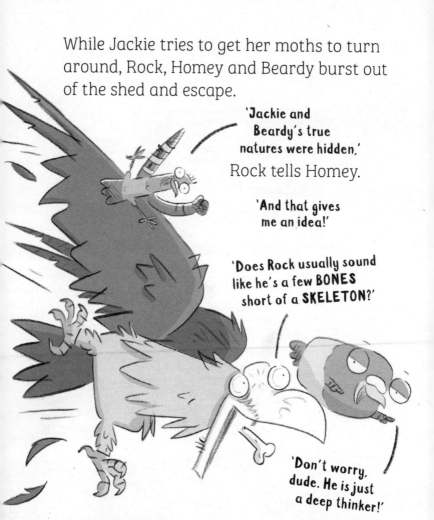

'Jackie and Beardy's true natures were hidden,' Rock tells Homey.

'And that gives me an idea!'

'Does Rock usually sound like he's a few **BONES** short of a **SKELETON**?'

'Don't worry, dude. He is just a deep thinker!'

Rock smiles. Because even though he can't be a **MASTER OF DISGUISE** right now, he's just worked out how to steal back the nest.

Beardy lies low in the barbecue again.

Rock and Homey find the **REAL PIGEONS**. 'The chimney's blocked!' says Tumbler, worried. 'What do we do now?'

'Don't worry,' says Rock. He explains his plan.

'Jackie Pigeon knows we're trying to steal the nest now! We'll have to be careful.'

The other pigeons bob their heads in agreement. Then they all sneak back inside the mansion.

'I'll meet up with you later, team.'

Jackie isn't back yet.
But they don't have
much time. Rock hides
behind a plant.

Homey dresses up as a
dog again and joins his
new friends.

'Hi, DOGGOS!
I need a favour.'

'Sure thing!'

The mission to get Beardy's nest back is about
to start. Rock gives the signal.

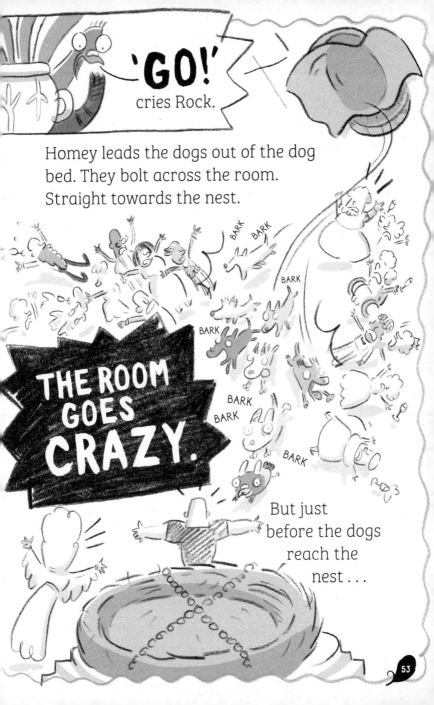

**'GO!'**
cries Rock.

Homey leads the dogs out of the dog bed. They bolt across the room. Straight towards the nest.

**THE ROOM GOES CRAZY.**

BARK BARK BARK BARK BARK BARK BARK BARK

But just before the dogs reach the nest . . .

53

. . . the lights go out.

The room is completely dark.

Someone screams.

'Ahhhhhhhhhh!'

'It must be
a black-out!'

'Is someone
stealing the
vulture's nest?'

What do you think is going on?

54

# CHAPTER 4

Finally, the back-up lights come on. They are dimmer than before.

Everyone is very confused.

'Good – the nest is still there.'

'Sorry I screamed – I'm scared of the dark.'

'Keep going!' shouts Rock. 'Towards the nest!'

Homey and the dogs start running again.

They're almost at the nest when someone steps in their way.

'STOP. RIGHT. THERE!'

It's Lady Twitcher. With Jackie Pigeon perched smugly on her head.

'My beautiful Jackie thinks you're trying to steal her nest,' says Lady Twitcher. 'What should we do with these naughty dogs, Jackie?'

Jackie Pigeon motions that they should kick the dogs out.

'Throw them out on the street?' says Lady Twitcher, wincing. 'That seems a bit mean.'

Jackie goes to pinch Lady Twitcher.

'OK, OK,' mutters Lady Twitcher. 'Whatever you say.'

Reginald steps forward. 'I've been waiting to throw these dogs out all day!'

Homey and the dogs yelp and jump back onto the bed, barking like mad.

But Reginald storms over and picks them up.

Marches them outside.

And throws the whole dog bed out into the backyard.

Is Rock's plan ruined?

'Whee!'

OOF!

Rock leaps out from his hiding spot. 'I guess you win, Jackie,' he says.

The moths fly Jackie across the room. 'You again!' she snarls.

'We **tried** to steal the nest back,' says Rock, with a cheeky grin.

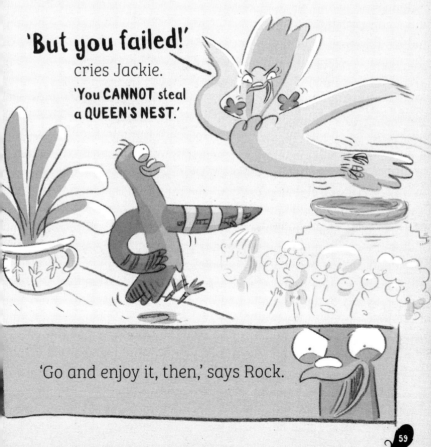

**'But you failed!'** cries Jackie. **'You CANNOT steal a QUEEN'S NEST.'**

'Go and enjoy it, then,' says Rock.

**'I WILL!'** laughs Jackie Pigeon.

She flies up
to the nest.

But hits
something hard.

Jackie is stunned.

She has flown into a
**PAINTING** of a nest.

**'THE NEST
IS GONE!'**

she screams.

'Things are not always what they seem,' says Rock. 'You gave me that idea!'

He explains what happened.

'When I gave the signal, Grandpouter cut the lights. Frillback brought the painting in from the shed.

'And Tumbler unlocked the padlock.'

Jackie searches the room desperately for the nest. It's nowhere to be found.

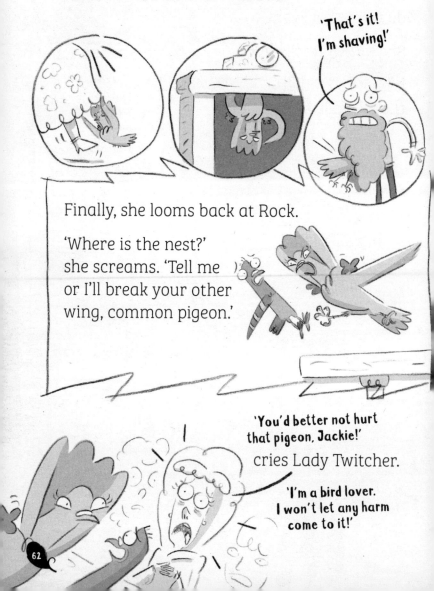

'That's it! I'm shaving!'

Finally, she looms back at Rock.

'Where is the nest?' she screams. 'Tell me or I'll break your other wing, common pigeon.'

'You'd better not hurt that pigeon, Jackie!' cries Lady Twitcher.

'I'm a bird lover. I won't let any harm come to it!'

Jackie sneers at Rock. 'She might be a bird lover. But I'm a **QUEEN**. And **QUEENS** do what they want.'

She **KICKS** Rock **HARD**.

It hurts so much that he falls back . . .

. . . through the air . . .

. . . but doesn't land on the ground. **Because Beardy Vulture catches him!**

'Thank you,' says Rock.

'You're welcome,' smiles Beardy.

Jackie Pigeon flies back to Lady Twitcher. But the human has finally had enough.

'I don't like anyone who hurts birds,' Lady Twitcher says.

'Reginald – get Jackie Pigeon out of here.'

And Jackie is suddenly thrown outside. To live with every other pigeon on the streets.

'This isn't over, common pigeons!' screams Jackie.

'I'll get my revenge on you all!'

Lady Twitcher crouches down to Beardy.
'You are very brave,' she says. 'Do you want to
come live with me? I love birds, you know!'

The vulture nods happily.

'Living on the top of a mountain can be
lonely,' Beardy says. 'I'll be happier here.'

Rock grins.

'Case closed, Trent!'
he says. 'Just one thing,'
says Beardy.
'Where IS my nest?'

Rock leads Beardy Vulture out into the backyard.

Where everyone is waiting.

With the dog bed.

Which was used to hide . . . **THE NEST!**

'Ta-dah!'

'We hid the nest under the rug when the lights were out,' explains Rock. 'It's safe and sound!'

'Amazing job!'

Lady Twitcher suddenly appears in the doorway.

'I've decided to dress like my new favourite birds – vultures! Now everyone come inside and enjoy the rest of the party!'

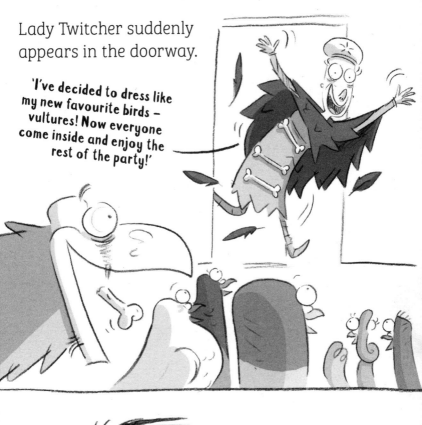

Rock might have a sore wing. But the case is solved. And he can still **PARTY HARD!**

**THE END . . . FOR NOW**

# UNFORTUNATELY . . .

## JACKIE PIGEON IS ANGRY.

'That was no way
to treat a QUEEN!'
she says. 'I'll just have
to start a new KINGDOM.'

She flies through
the streets, looking for
someone new to pinch.

'Hedgehogs
hurt to pinch.'

'Worms are
pinch-proof
because they're
so small.'

'HOW RUDE!'

Finally, Jackie flies down an alley and finds a stray cat. He has a bad attitude and teeth like nails. She lands on his head and pinches HARD and DEEP.

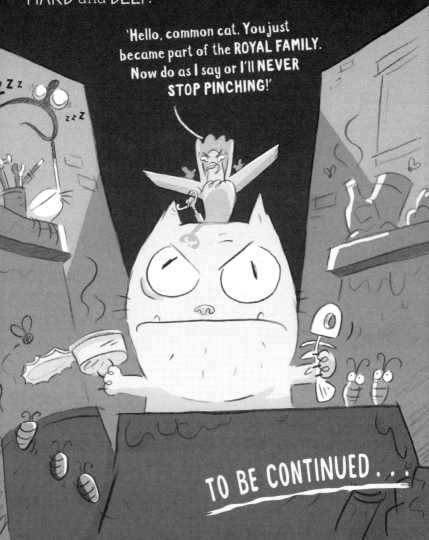

'Hello, common cat. You just became part of the ROYAL FAMILY. Now do as I say or I'll NEVER STOP PINCHING!'

TO BE CONTINUED . . .

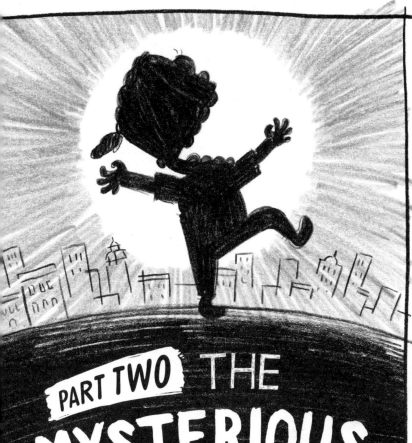

PART TWO THE **MYSTERIOUS KID X**

# CHAPTER 1

The **REAL PIGEONS** are settling down on the roof of their gazebo.

They are going to have a **roost**.

It's just like having a **nap**, but it sounds **WAY COOLER**.

*wiggle*

*wiggle*

'SNORE!'

'Happy **ROOSTING**, Trent!' says Rock.

Tumbler usually ties one of her legs to the gazebo. So she doesn't tumble away in her sleep.

But sometimes she forgets.

And rolls off the roof.

Taking all the sleeping pigeons down with her.

ZZz

If you have ever woken up in mid-air, you'll know how **SCARY** it is!

The pigeons flap their wings and come to a halt just above the ground.

'Whoops!'

Luckily, Rock's wing is better now.

'That's the third time this week that's happened,' says Grandpouter.

'And it's only Monday!' adds Frillback.

'We need to find a better way to **ROOST**,' says Rock.

He thinks about his favourite roosting spot when he lived on a farm. He always slept on the head of a llama.

'So comfy!'

'If Rock drools on me I'm going to headbutt the barnyard wall.'

Ever since they rescued Beardy Vulture's amazing nest, Rock has wanted one of his own.

'That's what I'll do,'

he announces eagerly.

'I'll build a special **REAL PIGEONS** nest!'

Rock is awesome at making disguises. But now he wants to be awesome at making other things. **BIGGER** things. Like nests!

So he flies off to find sticks – and some **STRINGY THINGS.**

The **REAL PIGEONS** let him know how they like to roost.

'I want to hang up-side down so I don't crush my feathers.'

'I like my body all twisty!'

'I like to dream about bread!'

'I like a surface where my **CROP** will be comfortable.'

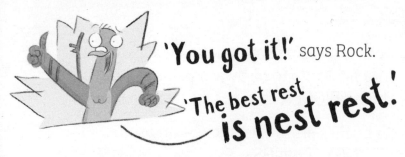

'**You got it!**' says Rock.

'**The best rest is nest rest.**'

They visit a nearby basketball court. There are no humans around. But plenty of sticks.

'How do you play basketball?'

'You just pretend the ball is a bird and make it fly.'

a stick!

another stick!

so many sticks!

Rock has collected everything he needs when someone yells.

'**HEY!**'

'This basketball court is MY home,' shouts a peacock, who is perched in a tree.

'Go away or suffer the consequences!'

Rock thinks the peacock looks like a turkey that got coloured in with blue and green crayons. Besides, the basketball court is for **EVERYONE**.

'We're not scared of you,' says Rock. 'Pigeons are only scared of crows.'

'And rain,' adds Frillback. 'It ruins my curls.'

'And **DO NOT FEED THE PIGEONS** signs,' adds Homey.

Rock ignores the peacock.

He puts Trent to one side so his favourite twig doesn't get built into the nest.

He pulls sticks this way . . .

. . . and that way.

He threads **STRINGY THINGS** everywhere . . .

. . . while the **REAL PIGEONS** watch from the sidelines.

When the nest is finished, Rock carries it up to the basketball ring.

'Ta-dah!'

llama head for Rock

twisty slide for Tumbler

loaf of bread to help Homey dream

in-built crop support for Grandpouter

swing for Frillback to hang upside down from

The pigeons look confused.

Rock has tried to give everyone a spot to roost. But it's a **MESS** of a nest.

'Did I build this right?'

'That isn't a **NEST!**' says the peacock. 'It's an **UGLY** hodge-podge of sticks. I'll bet it falls apart any minute now.'

Rock has a terrible feeling the peacock is right.

But Frillback defends him.

'Are you looking for a fight, peacock?' cries Frillback. 'You shouldn't pick on Rock. Because my feathers are pretty. Pretty **STRONG**, that is!'

The peacock smiles.

'How about a **STARING CONTEST** instead?' he says.

'**You're on!**' says Frillback.

The staring contest begins.

'There's no way I'm going to blink or look away!'

But the peacock has extra eyes.

'Now you are mine!'

Meanwhile, Homey has noticed something in the distance.

'Pigs?' he says.

'Don't panic, but there's a **BEAST** coming this way!'

The pigeons all look over. Frillback immediately loses the staring contest.

'I won! You looked away!'

The **BEAST** looks upset. Until she sees the pigeons.

Her face brightens, and
she runs straight for them.

She isn't just any kind of **BEAST**.

She's a **CHILD BEAST!**

But she's not looking
where she's going . . .

And she bangs into
the basketball pole.

**THUD!**

It shakes and the nest
falls to the ground.

**CRASH!**

'My nest!' cries Rock.

'I don't hate
to say I told
you so!'

The nest is destroyed. But the **CHILD BEAST** seems to be **OK**. And she runs towards the pigeons at full speed.

'PIDGIES!'

THE PIGEONS RUN FOR THEIR LIVES.

The **CHILD BEAST** is closing in.

She laughs and waves her arms like a dancing zombie.

'Why do kids chase birds?' puffs Rock.

'No-one knows!' answers Grandpouter. 'It's a mystery.'

The time for running is over. The pigeons fly off looking for safety.

GRAB
GRAB

Except for Rock, who digs a hole in the dirt.

'Hurry, Trent!!'

He ties a leaf to his foot and jumps in.

He has disguised himself as a **golf hole.**

FLAP
FLAP

But the **CHILD BEAST** saw.

She pulls Rock out and wraps her arms around him.

So **THAT'S** why kids always chase pigeons.

'They just want a hug!' wheezes Rock.

Rock looks around. Something is wrong.

There are no other humans in sight.

No humans **AT ALL**. Little kids aren't allowed out without an adult.

So where did this kid come from?

over here?

up here?

under here?

in here?

'Sometimes an **APPEARANCE** is more mysterious than a **DISAPPEARANCE!**' says Rock.

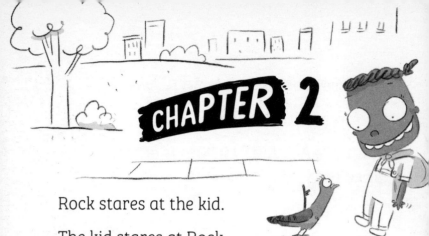

# CHAPTER 2

Rock stares at the kid.

The kid stares at Rock.

She is wearing a cute little cape with an X on it. Rock decides to call her **Kid X**. She must be lost.

'Hello, **PIDGIE**,' says **Kid X**, and points to Rock's twig. 'What's that?'

'This is Trent,' says Rock.

'I like DOLLS! Hello, TWIG DOLL!'

**Kid X** hugs Trent too.

They are all becoming fast friends.

Rock only knows a few things about kids.

Like how they ride in fancy cars.

'Nice wheels!'

And sing terrible music.

'WAAH!'

And sometimes have pet bears.

Luckily **Kid X** doesn't have a bear.

At that moment, the other pigeons reappear.

'**PIGS**, is it safe to be near a **CHILD BEAST?**' asks Homey.

'**Kid X** is harmless,' says Rock. 'But watch out, she is . . .'

'. . . a hugger.'

'**PIDGIE HUGS!**'

Humans don't actually understand pigeons. But Homey can't help asking **Kid X** a question anyway.

'Where is your family, kid?' he says.

**Kid X** grins. 'PIDGIE, you look like a tiny fridge!'

'FRIDGIE PIDGIE!'

food goes in here . . .

. . . and here.

Grandpouter decides to give **Kid X** a quick medical check-up.

'Say ahhhhhh.'

'She's perfectly healthy,' says Grandpouter.
'But why she's here by herself is a mystery.'

'I wish she hadn't broken my nest,' Rock says.
'Maybe I should make a stronger one.'

'Don't worry about that,' says Homey.
'We have to help **Kid X** find her family first.'

Rock knows Homey is right. Heroes always
help others first.

'REAL PIGEONS
HELP LOST KIDS!'

Kid X has a strange look on her face.

'Where **PIDGIE** teeth?' she asks.

'Pigeons don't have teeth,' says Rock. 'Probably because we'd look **RIDICULOUS**.'

'I think I know someone who can help us,' says Grandpouter suddenly.

The pigeons return to the peacock in the tree.

'Come back for a **STARING REMATCH**, have you?!'

'Did you see where this kid came from?' asks Grandpouter.

'No,' says the peacock.

But Rock has spotted something else.

'Look!'

DO NOT FEED THE PIGEONS

A nasty sign has appeared on the tree.

'Did you put this sign here?' demands Homey.

'No,' the peacock grins. 'I hope you do get fed. Because if you can't make a nest, you probably can't feed yourselves either.'

'We have to do **SOMETHING** about that sign!' cries Rock.

'Don't worry about it for now, **PIGS**,' says Homey. 'Getting Kid X back to her family is more important.'

Breadcrumbs are usually all Homey can think about. But not today. Rock is impressed.

All of a sudden, a basketball bounces onto the court.

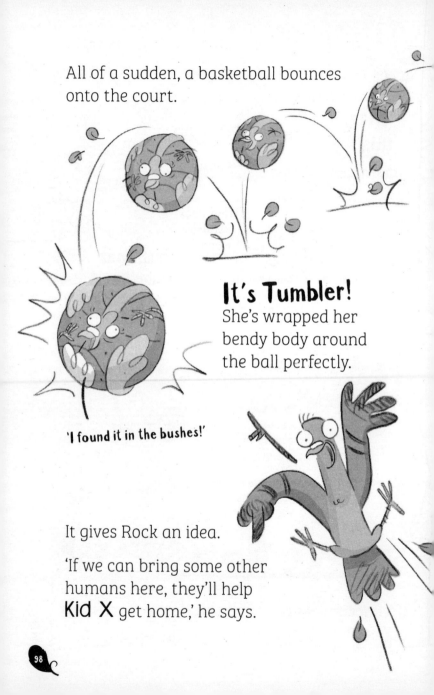

## It's Tumbler!
She's wrapped her bendy body around the ball perfectly.

'I found it in the bushes!'

It gives Rock an idea.

'If we can bring some other humans here, they'll help **Kid X** get home,' he says.

Tumbler bounces out of the basketball court and down the street.

Rock flies alongside her as a guide.

'Keep going straight, then turn left.'

'What does straight mean?'

They are looking for humans who can help **Kid X**.

They pass some butterflies.

'Yay!'

'Fun!'

They pass some dogs.

'Is that pigeon controlling a ball with just the power of his mind?'

99

Finally, Rock sees what they're after.
**Teenagers!**

Tumbler bounces over.

'Hey – that basketball is bouncing by itself!'

'It's a magic basketball!'

'Get it!'

The teenagers chase Tumbler through the streets.

All the way to the basketball court.

But the teenagers don't notice **Kid X**.

Instead they just *play basketball*.

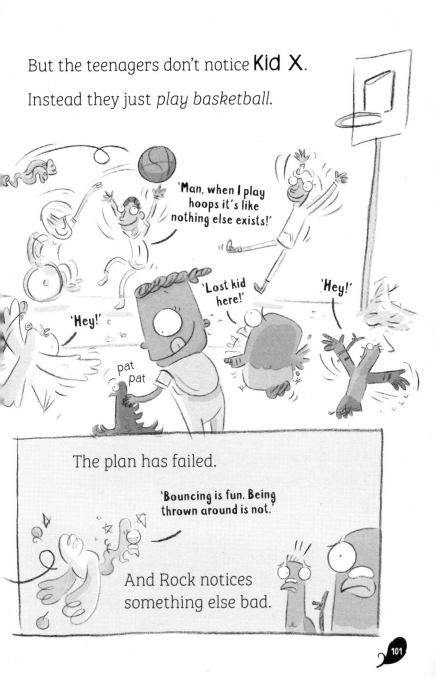

'Man, when I play hoops it's like nothing else exists!'

'Lost kid here!'

'Hey!'

'Hey!'

pat pat

The plan has failed.

'Bouncing is fun. Being thrown around is not.'

And Rock notices something else bad.

More signs have gone up while he was away.

DO NOT FEED THE PIGEONS

OR ELSE

YOU'RE NOT THEIR MOTHER

THEY'VE HAD ENOUGH ALREADY

'I didn't see who put them up,' says Grandpouter.

'But the peacock didn't move. It wasn't him.'

Rock is worried. He wonders if Jackie Pigeon is getting her revenge. But then again, she's a pigeon too!

'I am a QUEEN!!!'

'Forget the signs,' says Homey. '**Kid X** is crying!'

'I wanna go home,' sobs **Kid X**, wiping away tears. 'I'm sick of hiding. A **MONSTER** tried to get me! He had **NO** mouth!'

Rock imagines what this **MONSTER** might look like.

'Help me, Real Pigeons!'

cat head

sharp

no mouth

**Kid X** isn't just lost. She's running away from a horrible creature.

'We have to get **Kid X** back to her family **NOW**,' says Rock. 'Before this **MONSTER** finds her!'

# CHAPTER 3

Rock uses his **PIGEON POWER** to cheer **Kid X** up.

He dives into a bin and finds a plastic bag, some bubble gum and a lolly wrapper.

Rock Pigeon,
**MASTER OF
DISGUISE,**
has become
**Rock Doll.**

lolly
wrapper

gum

plastic
bag

The tears stop
running down
**Kid X**'s cheeks.

'I love you,
pidgie dolly!'

**Kid X** must have run away from the **MONSTER** and ended up at the basketball court.

It's up to the **REAL PIGEONS** to get her home.

'Let's fly around town,' says Rock. 'There must be other humans who will rescue her.'

'Good plan,' says Grandpouter. 'Frillback, carry **Kid X**!'

Frillback tries to lift her up.

But **Kid X** does **NOT** like being carried. And she throws a tantrum.

'No lift me! I HATE IT! PUT ME DOWN!'

They have been grounded.

But luckily, Rock has an idea.

'Come with me, squad,' he cries.

**Kid X** refuses to move, so Grandpouter stays behind with her.

Rock leads the others to a supermarket car park. And hops onto the handle of a shopping trolley.

**CARPARK**
**A PARK FOR CARS**

'Here we go!' he cries. 'We can take **Kid X** around town in this special **KID CAR**!'

Meanwhile, the others are exploring.

Homey watches shoppers go to their cars.

'I don't believe in bags. Food should be carried in stomachs!'

And Tumbler finds a fancy pair of glasses on the ground.

'Someone must have dropped these,' says Tumbler. 'They make everything look HUGE!'

The squad takes the trolley back to the basketball court. **Kid X** climbs straight in.

'Push me, **PIDGIES**, push me!'

Tumbler looks closely at **Kid X** through her new glasses. She can see three things.

pizza sauce

snot

toothpaste

'It's not unusual for kids to be covered in snot and toothpaste,' says Tumbler. 'But the pizza sauce looks fresh.'

Rock twists **Kid X's** cape around.

'This isn't a cape,' he says. 'It's a bib! She had it on backwards.'

'There's a pizza parlour near the supermarket,' cries Homey. '**Kid X** must have been eating there with her family before she ran away. Let's go to the pizza parlour, PIGS! This way, Frillback!'

Frillback gets behind the shopping trolley. And they push off.

'**Wheeeeeee!**'

As the pigeons leave with **Kid X**, the peacock blows a raspberry.

# ppppttt!!

Suddenly, the teenagers notice them.

'Hey, those birds have kidnapped a kid!'

one of them yells.

'**Get them!**'

Oh no! The teenagers have it all wrong!

They chase the trolley across the court.

'You had your chance to save the day!' cries Rock.

Through the park.

'Those BIG KIDS are scary!'

And over a bridge.

Until the trolley hits a tree root and tips over.

'AAAAAAH!'

# CRASH!

The teenagers rush to the crashed trolley.

But the pigeons – and **Kid X** – are gone.

'Is that a bubblegum wig?'

'Huh?'

They're flying for the treetop.

'PUT ME DOWN! I HATE IT!'

The **REAL PIGEONS** and **Kid X** sit helplessly in the treetop.

They can't fly away without **Kid X** throwing another tantrum. And any minute now, the teenagers will see them in the tree.

THE REAL PIGEONS ARE TRAPPED!

'When we find those pigeons, I'm going to teach them a lesson!'

# CHAPTER 4

'Maybe we should fly off and leave **Kid X** with the teenagers?' says Rock.

**'NO WAY, PIG!'** cries Homey. 'She's scared of them. We need to get her back to the pizza parlour, to her family!'

'You're right,' admits Rock. 'Actually, I have a better idea.'

He goes back to the basketball court. He collects the sticks from his broken nest.

Rock works quickly. But he isn't fixing the nest to roost in.

'We need a nest that suits crime-fighters,' says Rock. 'Because **REAL PIGEONS** don't just nest . . .

# 'REAL PIGEONS
# NEST HARD!'

Rock has built a **NEST PLANE**.

It flies beautifully.

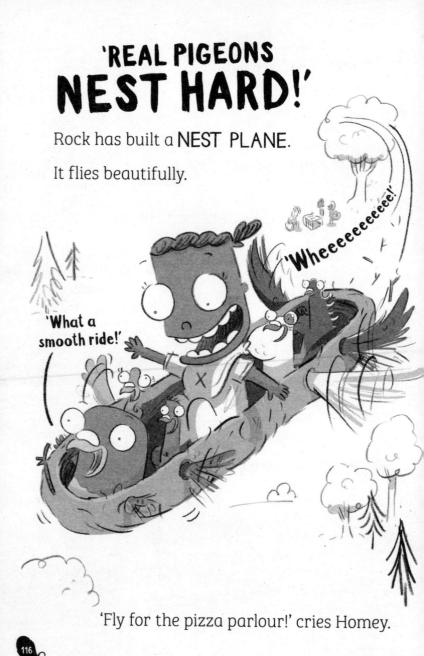

'Fly for the pizza parlour!' cries Homey.

Rock looks over the edge of the **NEST PLANE** and sees something shocking.

More bad signs! How did they get onto the plane?

DO NOT FEED THE PIGEONS

THEY NEVER SAY THANK YOU!

ALL PIGEONS ARE PICKPOCKETS

Whoever is putting them up is getting closer and closer to the **REAL PIGEONS**.

Rock starts to feel scared.

The **REAL PIGEONS** have defeated lots of villains. Any of them could be returning for revenge.

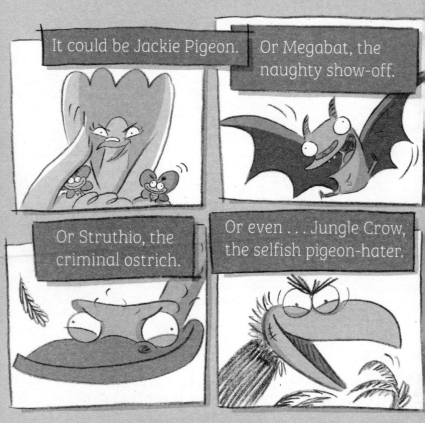

It could be Jackie Pigeon.

Or Megabat, the naughty show-off.

Or Struthio, the criminal ostrich.

Or even . . . Jungle Crow, the selfish pigeon-hater.

Rock gulps. He doesn't like to think about so many villains at once!

Homey aims the **NEST PLANE** at the street below.

The pizza parlour is right there.

'You're almost there, Kid X!'

Rock looks closely. There are no crows, bats, ostriches or evil pigeons down on the street. But there are humans.

'There are those kidnapping pigeons!'

It's the teenagers. And they've gathered a crowd.

Rock knows they can't just fly down, because the humans will grab them. So he turns to Tumbler.

'Let's try our basketball plan,' Rock says. 'But do it differently this time. If you know what I mean!'

Tumbler's eyes widen.

She jumps out of the **NEST PLANE** and grabs the basketball from the teenagers.

'I sure do!'

'Time to play BALL!'

Tumbler bounces from human to human.

She bounces on people's toes.

She bops heads.

She cannons into tummies.

'OW!'

BOP

'BURP!'

The humans scatter.

'Flee!'

'RUN!'

Finally, the **NEST PLANE** lands on the street. But the pizza parlour is **CLOSED!**

CLOSED

They've hit a **dead end**. The pizza trail has gone cold.

DENTIST
X
DR XANADU

'What now?' says Homey.

Rock looks at the shop next door, and remembers two important things.

'Where PIDGIE teeth?'

'This isn't a cape! It's a bib!'

'Squad, follow me!' he says.

Rock takes them all inside the shop next door.

'Oh no!' cries **Kid X**, with a tremble.
'It's the **MONSTER** with no mouth!'

Except it's not actually a **MONSTER**.

## It's a dentist.

'Well, if my name
isn't **Dr Xanadu**!'

WHIZ
WHIZ

From behind the dentist, two big
humans rush forward.

'We've been looking
everywhere for you!'

GRAB GRAB

GRAB

GRAB

The mystery is solved. The pigeons have found **Kid X**'s family. Her parents hug her tightly.

Homey is so happy he's in tears.

'I'm just so glad she's back with her family!' he says.

'Is everything OK, Homey?' says Rock.

'I haven't seen my own family in a long time,' says Homey, blowing his nose on his feathers. 'But I'm glad **Kid X** found hers!'

Rock gives Homey a big hug. Even though he's covered in pigeon snot.

Kid **X** is still scared of the dentist. And the adults have noticed.

So the pigeons do one more thing to help **Kid X**.

They keep her company while the dentist cleans her teeth.

The pigeons say their final farewells.

But Rock hears a banging coming from outside.

He marches off to investigate.

'Bye, fridgie pidgie!'

BANG! BANG! BANG!

And catches the creature who has been nailing up the bad signs.

# IT'S FRILLBACK!

DO NOT FEED PIGEONS

Frillback drops the sign and hammer.

'What are you **DOING?**' cries Rock.

Frillback doesn't answer.
Her beak trembles.
She doesn't seem to
be herself. In fact, she's
been **very** quiet today.

Rock takes a good close look at her.
Her eyes aren't right.

'You've been
**HYPNOTISED!**'
Rock gasps.

'Poor Frillback!'

Rock and the pigeons help Frillback into the **NEST PLANE**.

And together, they fly her back to the basketball court.

'Excuse me! Hypnotised pigeon coming through!'

Where the peacock laughs at them.

'I told you to go away or else,' he says. 'You didn't listen. So I hypnotised your friend during our **STARING CONTEST**, to make her put up those scary signs.'

'You scared me plenty,' says Rock. 'I thought someone was taking revenge on us!'

'Now please un-hypnotise our friend!' says Grandpouter sternly. 'And we'll **ASK** next time we want to visit the basketball court.'

'**Fine**,' the peacock says, and clicks his foot.

CLICK!

Frillback shakes her head.

'**I'm so sorry!**' she says.

'I couldn't stop myself from putting up signs.'

'You're back!'

The **REAL PIGEONS** fly their awesome nest back to their gazebo.

'A UFO!'

'RUN FOR YOUR LIVES!'

IT HAS BEEN A **BUSY DAY.**

And before they even get out of the **NEST PLANE,** they all fall asleep.

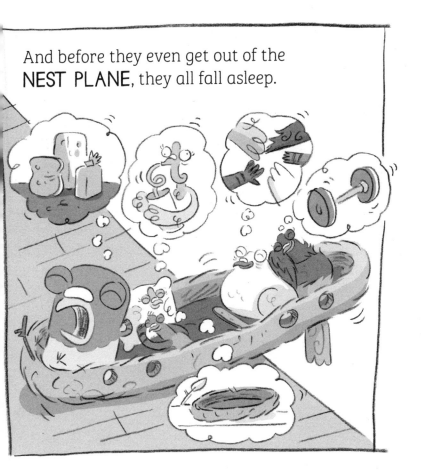

It turns out any kind of **NEST** is good for a **ROOST**. If Rock were awake, he'd probably be really proud of himself.

THE END . . . FOR NOW

# IT'S SAD...

## ...THAT HOMEY HASN'T SEEN HIS FAMILY FOR SO LONG.

But that very night, a photograph floats slowly down a nearby creek.

It shows some pigeons – all tied up.

They look *very* familiar.

And it looks like they're in trouble!

If only Homey knew . . .

TO BE CONTINUED . . .

PART THREE

# HOME SWEET HOMEY

# CHAPTER 1

Rock Pigeon wakes up with a start.

'GASP!'

There is a low rumbling noise nearby.
And it's getting louder.

RUMBLE
RUMBLE

Is there a **MONSTER** coming to get them?

'Can you hear that noise, squad?' says Rock.

# RUMBLE
## RUMBLE

RUMBLE RUMBLE

But it's not a monster.

The pigeons are just **SUPER** hungry.

'RUMBLE RUMBLE
is **TUMMY TALK**
for **FEED ME!**'
says Homey.

No-one understands tummies like Homey.

Grandpouter sends the pigeons off to collect food.

Rock and Frillback collect seeds.

'Ten will be enough.'

Tumbler collects sultanas.

'Ten will be enough.'

Homey collects loaves of bread.

'Will ten be enough?'

The pigeons all bring their food back to the **NEST PLANE**. They are about to dig into an almighty breakfast . . . when a spoonbill called Bill Spoon drops by.

'Hi, gang!' says Bill. 'I found a strange photo at the pond this morning. Thought you might be interested.'

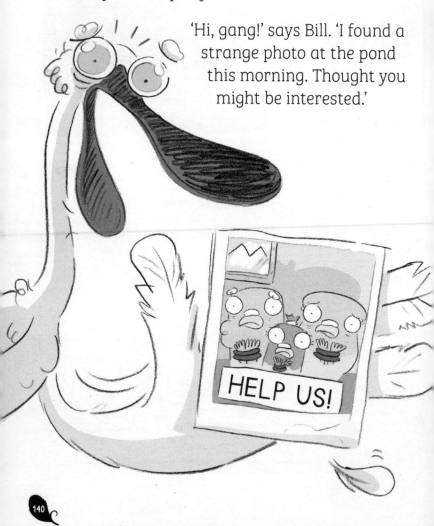

HELP US!

Homey takes one look at the photo and drops his bread in shock.

'That's my **FAMILY**!' he cries.

'They're in trouble!'

HELP US!

Someone has taken Homey's family hostage!

'Oh no, Homey!' cries Tumbler.

She wraps him in a **BELT HUG** – firm, comfortable and all the way around.

hug

hug

'Apparently these photos are everywhere!' says Bill Spoon.

MEANWHILE, IN ANTARCTICA . . .

'Huh?'

MEANWHILE, IN MEXICO . . .

'I made one of those photos into a hat!'

'Nice one, Clark.'

MEANWHILE, AT A NEARBY BASKETBALL COURT . . .

'I challenge you to a STARING CONTEST!'

142

'Thanks Bill,' says Rock. 'We'd better go save Homey's family!'

'I'm going to do some **PIDGE-JITSU** on whoever has done this!' cries Frillback.

# 'REAL PIGEONS RESCUE HOMEY'S FAMILY!'

'It's time to use your **PIGEON POWER** and lead us to your family, Homey!' says Grandpouter.

But Homey doesn't say anything. He just looks at the photo. A single pigeon tear splashes down on it.

'What's the matter?' asks Rock.

'Sorry, PIGS,' says Homey. 'I have no idea where my family is.'

Rock scratches his head with his twig, Trent.

Then he scratches Trent (just in case Trent is itchy).

**'But aren't you a HOMING PIGEON, Homey?'** Rock asks.

Homey sighs. 'The truth is that I know how to fly anywhere in the world. Except for one place – my family's home.'

Homey explains.

'My family are all homing pigeons.'

Dad (Homer)

Mum (Hominy)

Sister (Hombellina)

Me (Homey)

'But I don't remember them much. I last saw them when I was a baby, right before I went flying by myself for the first time.'

'My homing skills weren't properly developed. And I got lost. I searched for ages but I never found my way home again.'

'Sis?'

'Dad?'

'Mum?'

'I missed my family heaps. So when I found some loaves of bread on the street, I adopted them as my new family.'

'That's messed up!'

'Eventually my bread family started going mouldy,' sighs Homey. 'So I ate them. And tried to forget about home.'

'That's REALLY messed up!'

'So we **CAN'T** rescue your family,' says Tumbler, 'because we don't know where they are?'

Homey nods.

Rock puts a wing around his friend.

'**REAL PIGEONS** are **REAL FIGHTERS!**' he says. 'We'll find a way to save your family. But you can't fight crime on an empty stomach. So let's eat!'

The pigeons all offer Homey their bread to cheer him up.

'Thanks, **PIGS**,' says Homey, taking a bite.

Straight away, his eyes fill with water.
He opens his beak to burp.
But fire shoots out.

'FLAME-URRRRRP!'

Rock takes a close look at
the bread. 'This bread has
**chilli** in it!' he cries.

hot
chillies!

Pigeons should **STAY AWAY** from hot things.

Like **cement** on a warm day.

'My feet are burning!'

And **chimney** tops.

'My outsides are burning!'

And, of course, **chilli peppers.**

'My insides are burning!'

'Who would put chilli in bread?' cries Homey.

Before anyone can answer, he sneezes.

Chilli doesn't just burn.
It can also make you sneeze!

While the others comfort Homey, Rock notices something interesting in the photo.

'Squad! I think
I've found a clue!'

'There's a mountain with two peaks in the photo,' says Rock. 'So Homey's family must be close to it.'

'I know that mountain,' says Homey.

'Come on, squad,' cries Rock. 'Let's get this rescue mission off the ground!'

'Good luck, pigeons!'

'A-COO!'

# CHAPTER 2

The pigeons take off in the **NEST PLANE**.
Homey sneezes and points the way.

They fly through sunshine.

'A-COO!'

Rain.

Migrating geese.

'A-COO!'

And snow.

'Are you sure we're flying the right way?' says Frillback, after a while.

'No,' sighs Homey. 'I think sneezing has messed up my sense of direction.'

The **REAL PIGEONS** are lost. It's getting late. And they're no closer to finding Homey's family.

'**I know where we are,**' says Rock, looking around.

'That farm looks familiar. Let's make a stop.'

'Hoot!'

The pigeons land on a couple of pigs.

It's the farm where Rock grew up.
He's excited to pay everyone a visit.

'Hello, everyone,' cries Rock. 'Guess what –
I'm a crime-fighter now! And I have a twig!
Say hi to Trent!'

Homey sees a breadcrumb on the ground.

But this bread has chilli in it too.

It seems like there is chilli bread **EVERYWHERE**.

Grandpouter takes Homey to visit some cows. 'Milk helps wash that chilli taste away!' he explains.

'Thanks, cows!' cries Homey.

'How unusual.'

'Time to go again!' yawns Homey. 'We have to be **RESCUE PIGEONS!**'

But Grandpouter shakes his head. 'It's very late,' he says. 'I know you're worried about your family, but let's get some sleep. We'll head off first thing.'

Rock takes them to the llamas.

'This used to be my favourite sleeping spot. Llamas are even comfier than nests!'

The pigeons wrap themselves in llama ears and fall asleep.

The next morning, just as the sun is rising, a rooster throws back its head to crow.

But its head comes off.

Now it's time for the **REAL PIGEONS** to find Homey's family.

Homey is feeling much better today. He guides the pigeons over valleys and small towns.

Until they finally reach the mountain with two peaks. And they see something amazing.

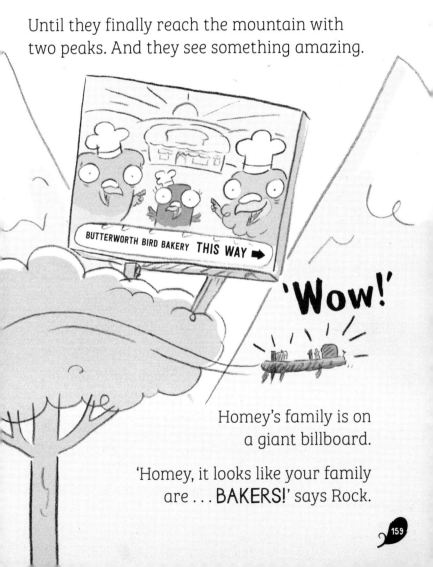

BUTTERWORTH BIRD BAKERY **THIS WAY** ➡

'Wow!'

Homey's family is on a giant billboard.

'Homey, it looks like your family are ... **BAKERS!**' says Rock.

Homey is overjoyed.

'No wonder I love bread so much!' he cries.

'Makes perfect sense!'

'We should check the bakery for clues,' says Rock.

The pigeons arrive at the bakery and park the **NEST PLANE**.

'This place looks familiar.'

But it's obvious that things are **NOT RIGHT**.

**MEGABREAD**

Because there is a different sign on the building.

161

A pack of **CATS** run out of the bakery, hissing and snorting.

HISS    HISS

SNORT

And standing on the head of the biggest cat ...

PINCH    PINCH

... is Jackie, **THE EVIL PIGEON!**

The **REAL PIGEONS** shiver in the tree.

Jackie Pigeon was already dangerous. But now that she is controlling a **CAT PACK** with her claws, she is an even bigger threat!

'I am **QUEEN** of the **CATS**,' Jackie cries. 'Now don't make me get pinchy! Get to work!'

'Yes, your Meow-jesty!'

PINCH

PINCH

The cats run off into the distance.

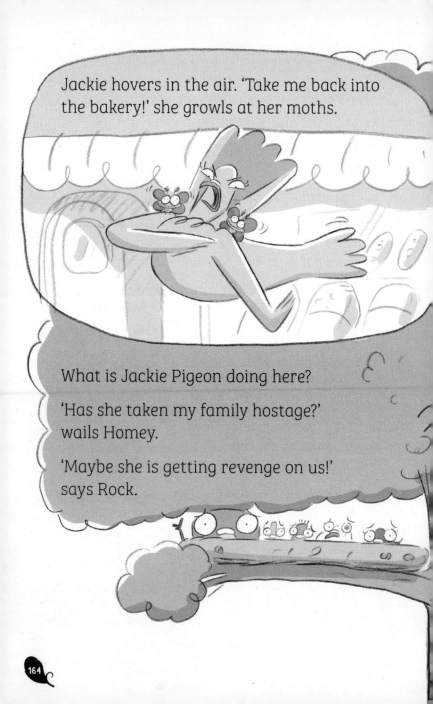

Jackie hovers in the air. 'Take me back into the bakery!' she growls at her moths.

What is Jackie Pigeon doing here?

'Has she taken my family hostage?' wails Homey.

'Maybe she is getting revenge on us!' says Rock.

Rock only knows one thing for sure.

'We **HAVE** to get inside that bakery!' he cries.
'But we'll need disguises, so that Jackie
doesn't recognise us.'

'I'm sure we can think
up good disguises if we put
our heads together,'
says Tumbler.

'And maybe
our bodies too,'
says Rock.

'That gives
me an idea!'

Rock explains his plan.

The **REAL PIGEONS**
huddle together.
And get all tangled up.

Until they are in position.

And look just like . . .

Since Rock is the MASTER OF DISGUISE, he explains HOW TO BE AN OWL.

They walk into the bakery and are shocked to see four very familiar faces.

JUNGLE CROW!

STRUTHIO OSTRICH!

MEGABAT!

AND JACKIE PIGEON TOO!

Why are all these villains here?

168

# CHAPTER 3

'Welcome to our bakery,' says Jungle Crow. 'Who are you?'

Homey is the head of the owl. Which means he needs to talk. But being close to so many villains has made him nervous!

**'OWL!'** he says suddenly.
**'Not a pigeon!'**

Has Homey given the squad away?

'Al Notapigeon?
That's a weird name,'
says Jungle Crow.
But then he smiles.
'It's nice to meet you, Al.'

The villains have taken over the bakery!
Homey's family must be in here somewhere.

But why would villains want to make *bread*?
They could be doing **MUCH** more evil things.

Homey clears his throat.

'Could I have a tour?
Then I will eat some
bread. Or a mouse.
Or some mouse bread.'

'A tour?' says Jungle Crow.

'Just do it,' says Jackie.

'Don't tell me what to do!'

'The more people who know about our bread, the better,' grins Megabat.

'HURRY UP,' says Struthio Ostrich.

'TOUR TIME!'

'OK, OK,' says Jungle Crow. 'Follow me, Al.' They go into the back of the bakery.

'This is where we make our **MEGABREAD!**' says Jungle Crow. 'It's a new kind of bread. Struthio Ostrich kneads the dough with his head.'

'**HEAD STRONG**,' says Struthio. '**BREAD BONK!**'

'That's a giant ball of dough!'

'I love dough! It's basically baby bread!'

'I work the oven,' says Jungle Crow.

'Megabat is our mascot,' Jungle Crow explains. 'He puts labels on the loaves.'

'And Jackie Pigeon sends the bread out into the world.'

Homey normally loves bread-talk. But right now he just wants to find his family.

'Before we go on, I need to get these loaves out of the oven, Al,' says Jungle Crow.

'This is our chance,' whispers Rock. 'Let's go look for Homey's family.'

'Great tour,'
    says Homey.

'But I think I saw a mouse outside. Gotta go, dudes!'

The pigeons pretend to leave the bakery. But as soon as they're out of sight, they separate to search for the kidnapped bakers.

Tumbler looks in the cupboards.

Grandpouter searches in the flour.

COUGH
COUGH

Frillback checks the freezer.

Rock and Homey hear scratching noises coming from behind a door.

They dart in to find . . .

Homey and Rock untie the hostages.
And they leap on Homey in joy.

'FAMILY PIGS!'
cries Homey.

'Homey??'

'Brother!'

'Where did you go?
We thought we'd
lost you forever!'

He has finally found his family!

'We found one of your photos!' Homey says.

'I knew that if we kept slipping them out the window, someone would rescue us,' says his dad, Homer. 'But I never dreamed our rescuer would be you, Homestead Butterworth!'

'Who is **Homestead Butterworth**?' asks Rock.

'That's Homey!' says his mum. 'Homey is short for Homestead.'

Yet this is no time for a reunion. Rock tries to open the window but it's rusted in place.

'Pull, Trent!'

'We need to get out of here,' he says. 'Before those villains discover us.'

'Let's use our PIGEON POWERS!'

says Homey's family.

'I have **X-ray vision**,' says Hominy.

NOT READY

ALMOST READY

'I can fly super fast,' says Hombellina.

SEEDS

'And I get visions that predict the future,' says Homer. 'Like with the photos. In fact, I had a slightly worrying vision about the **REAL PIGEONS**. And you were in it, Rock.'

'What do you mean?'

But before Homer can explain, the other pigeons burst into the room.

'They saw us!'

'They're coming!'

'Quick! Back into disguise!'

The pigeons become Al Notapigeon again just as the villains appear.

But Homey has forgotten the feathers that look like ears.

Struthio steps forward.
'NICE COSTUME — FAKE OWL!'

'Hoot?'

He kicks Al Notapigeon in the tummy and the pigeons separate.

THEY HAVE BEEN EXPOSED!

# CHAPTER 4

'So **Al Notapigeon** actually is pigeons,' sneers Jungle Crow. 'Your time is UP, REAL PIGEONS!'

PINCH

PINCH

184

Jackie's cats crawl into the room.

The pigeons are **COMPLETELY** surrounded by danger.

Jungle Crow breaks a breadstick in half and tosses it into his beak.

Jungle Crow is bad. But Rock doesn't want him to suffer.

'Don't eat that!' cries Rock. 'It's chilli bread!'

185

'I KNOW,' laughs Jungle Crow, swallowing. 'Megabread is **chilli bread.** Crows can eat chilli without a problem. But pigeons can't – haha!'

Jungle Crow used to be behind bars, but he explains that he and Megabat escaped their cage.

And started an **ANTI-PIGEON CLUB.**

ANTI-PIGEON CLUB

FIRST MEETING: THIS TUESDAY

BRING A PLATE OF FOOD

Struthio escaped his ostrich farm to join the club.

And Jackie couldn't resist either.

'Our revenge was making bread you can't eat!' cries Jungle Crow.

So that's why the villains have taken over Homey's family's bakery.

'I'm also here hoping to get famous,' adds Megabat.

Jackie leans forward, her eyes glowing with madness. 'But now our revenge will be final. I'll feed you to my cats!'

IS THIS IT FOR THE REAL PIGEONS SQUAD?

'ENOUGH!' cries Homey. 'You've taken over this bakery. You've tied up my family. And you've even RUINED BREAD.

'STOP IT NOW!'

'Or what?' laughs Jungle Crow. 'You'll give me bad directions? You're a **homing pigeon**. What can you possibly do to scare me?'

Homey grins. **'I can EAT!'**

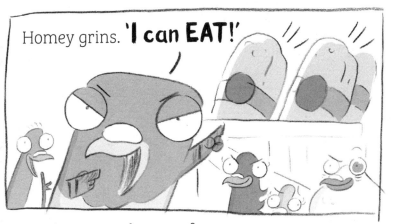

He shoves ten loaves of **chilli bread** into his beak.

'Here we go!'

Homey's eyes water.

Smoke pours out of his ears.

He opens his beak and . . .

'FLAME

Homey breathes fire at the villains and the cats. It's total chaos!

'My brother is a fire-breather!'

The other pigeons escape!

But then Homey runs out of fire breath.

The villains turn back. 'Get him!' Jungle Crow cries.

RUMBLE
RUMBLE

'What's that rumbling noise?'

'It's not a tummy this time!'

A giant ball of bread dough rolls into the
room. It's **PIGEONS** to the rescue!

RUMBLE

RUMBLE

The dough collects all the villains . . .

. . . and **SMASHES** through the wall to the outside.

'What should we do with all these villains and cats?' asks Rock.

'Get them out of my sight!' says Homey.

'A-COO!'

'I can do that,' grins Frillback.

And she kicks the ball high into the sky.

'NOOOOOOOOOOOOO!'

Homey thrusts a wing in the air.

'I declare the era of **chilli bread OVER!**' he says. 'Now my family can be bakers again!'

# THE PIGEONS ALL CHEER.

'Good kick!'

'Hooray!' cries Rock. 'Now let's go home, Homey.'

But Homey shakes his head. 'I'm sorry, PIGS. I want to stay with my family and learn how to be a baker. But that means I'll have to quit the **REAL PIGEONS** squad.'

The **REAL PIGEONS** start to tear up.

But then Hombellina has an idea.

'Why don't you all spend the summer here? We'll teach Homey how to bake. And after that you can fight crime again!'

'Great idea, little **PIG**,' says Homey.

'Did my brother just call me a **PIG**?' says Hombellina.

'Still happy he found you?' Frillback winks.

Rock finds a baker's hat.

And gives it to Homey.

'What are you waiting for?' says Rock.
**'LET'S BAKE!'**

**THE END**

# HAPPILY...

## THE REAL PIGEONS ENJOY THEIR SUMMER.

Homey learns all the family secrets.

Tumbler and Hombellina become friends.

'Woocoo!'

And they have a big chilli bonfire.

'Live by the flame, die by the flame, MegaBread!'

'Homey, are you eating all of today's bread?'

But something is still bothering Rock.

So he finds Homey's dad.

'You said you had a worrying vision about the squad, Homer,' Rock says. 'What did you see?'

Homer sighs. 'You're not going to like it.'

But Rock needs to know.

'Please tell me!'

'Very well,' says Homer. 'The REAL PIGEONS squad will END, and it will END soon!'

'GASP!'

# INVENTOR STATEMENTS

'The best thing about using a **BONE STRAW** is that you can eat the **BONE** when you're done drinking!'
- B. Vulture

'Use a **BONE STRAW** next time you order a shake. And don't think too much about where the bone came from in the first place.'
- L. Twitcher

## #BONESTRAWS

# DID YOU KNOW

## REAL
# PiGEONS
### ARE
## REAL-LIFE
### PIGEONS ?

### ROCK PIGEON

The most common pigeon in the world. Grey with two black stripes on each wing. Very good at blending in!

### FRILLBACK PIGEON

Known as a 'fancy pigeon'. Humans have bred them to be covered in curly feathers. These birds don't need to use hair curlers!

### TUMBLER PIGEON

Known to tumble or somersault while in flight. They fly normally before unexpectedly doing aerial acrobatics.

### HOMING PIGEON

Has the incredible ability to fly long distances and return home from very far away. They were used to deliver letters many years ago.

### POUTER PIGEON

The big bubble that looks like a chest is actually called a crop. They store food in their crops before releasing it to their stomachs. Yuk!

## FIND OUT MORE AT REALPIGEONS.COM!

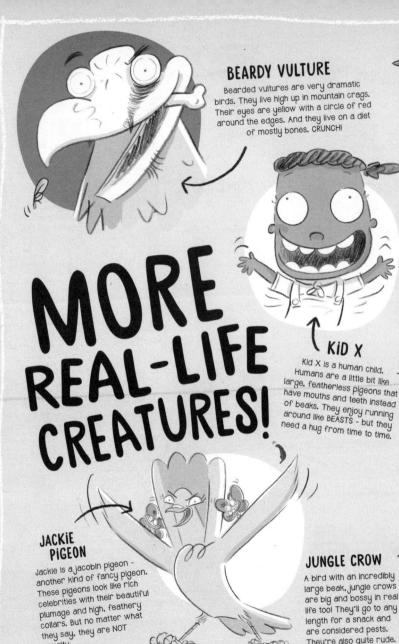

## BEARDY VULTURE

Bearded vultures are very dramatic birds. They live high up in mountain crags. Their eyes are yellow with a circle of red around the edges. And they live on a diet of mostly bones. CRUNCH!

# MORE REAL-LIFE CREATURES!

## KID X

Kid X is a human child. Humans are a little bit like large, featherless pigeons that have mouths and teeth instead of beaks. They enjoy running around like BEASTS - but they need a hug from time to time.

## JACKIE PIGEON

Jackie is a jacobin pigeon - another kind of fancy pigeon. These pigeons look like rich celebrities with their beautiful plumage and high, feathery collars. But no matter what they say, they are NOT royalty.

## JUNGLE CROW

A bird with an incredibly large beak, jungle crows are big and bossy in real life too! They'll go to any length for a snack and are considered pests. They're also quite rude.

## STRAW NECK IBIS

Ibises used to only hang out in wetlands, but they've learned to live in cities too where they enjoy eating out of bins. They look like small leftover dinosaurs but they're actually pretty smart!

## PEACOCK

Peacock is actually just the male name for a peafowl. Girls are called 'peahens' and babies are called 'peachicks' (cute!). An average peacock will have over two hundred tail feathers with spots on each one. That's a lot of fake eyes!

## MEGABAT

Megabats are great at smelling things - that's how they locate fruit at night when they gather for dinner parties in fruit trees. True to their name, some megabats are really big with a wingspan of up to 1.7 metres. Now that's mega!

## STRUTHIO OSTRICH

Ostriches swallow rocks to help break up food in their stomachs so that they can digest correctly. It's strange but also pretty clever, since they don't have teeth!

# HAVE YOU READ ALL THE

## REAL PIGEONS'

### ADVENTURES? NO?

## WHAT ARE YOU WAITING FOR, YOUR FEATHERS TO GROW?

**BOOK ONE**

Rock and his mystery-solving pigeon pals tackle their first caseload:

WHY HAVE ALL THE BREADCRUMBS DISAPPEARED?

WHO ON EARTH IS KIDNAPPING BATS?

AND CAN THEY AVERT A
## DINNER DISASTER??

A series of mysteries threatens to tear apart the pigeon squad:

**BOOK TWO**

WHO IS BOTTLING BIRDS?

HOW DID A DERANGED OSTRICH ESCAPE HIS OSTRICH FARM?

AND WHAT IS THE PIE MAKER'S **DARK SECRET?**

**BOOK THREE**

Rock wants to make a perfect nest for the squad, but investigations keep getting in the way:

WHO HAS STOLEN A VULTURE'S NEST?

HOW DID A BEASTLY CHILD GET LOST IN A PARK?

AND WILL HOMEY EVER FIND HIS **LONG-LOST FAMILY?**

# REAL PIGEONS

## HOW TO DRAW HOMEY

DRAW HOMEY!

# REAL PIGEONS

## HOW TO DRAW TUMBLER

DRAW TUMBLER!

FOR LEIGH MCDONALD – ANDREW
FOR JACQUIE, MATT, OLLIE AND ISSY – BEN

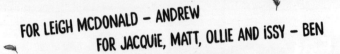

# REAL PIGEONS
## NEST HARD

first published in 2019
Hardie Grant Children's Publishing

This edition published in 2022 by Farshore

An imprint of HarperCollins*Publishers*
1 London Bridge Street
London SE1 9GF

HarperCollins*Publishers*
1st Floor, Watermarque Building,
Ringsend Road, Dublin 4, Ireland

farshore.co.uk

Text copyright © 2019 Andrew McDonald
Illustration copyright © 2019 Ben Wood
Series design copyright © 2019 Hardie Grant Children's Publishing
Design by Kristy Lund-White

ISBN 978 0 7555 0137 3

Printed and bound in the UK using 100% renewable
electricity at CPI Group (UK) Ltd

1

A CIP catalogue record for this title is available from the British Library

Stay safe online. Any website addresses listed in this book are correct at the time of going
to print. However, Farshore is not responsible for content hosted by third parties. Please be
aware that online content can be subject to change and websites can contain content that is
unsuitable for children. We advise that all children are supervised when using the internet.

MIX
Paper from
responsible sources
FSC™ C007454

This book is produced from independently certified FSC™ paper
to ensure responsible forest management.

For more information visit: www.harpercollins.co.uk/green